ALSO BY JULES FEIFFER

Cartoons

Sick, Sick, Sick
Passionella and Other Stories
The Explainers
Boy, Girl, Boy, Girl
Hold Me!
Feiffer's Album
The Unexpurgated Memoirs of Bernard Mergendeiler
Feiffer on Civil Rights
Feiffer's Marriage Manual
Feiffer on Nixon: The Cartoon Presidency

Novels

Harry, The Rat with Women
Ackroyd

Memoir

The Great Comic Book Heroes

Plays

Little Murders
The White House Murder Case
Knock, Knock

Screenplay

Carnal Knowledge

Drawings

Pictures at a Prosecution

TANTRUM

Jules Feiffer

Alfred A. Knopf, New York, 1979

THIS IS A BORZOI BOOK
PUBLISHED BY ALFRED A. KNOPF, INC.

Copyright © 1979 by Jules Feiffer
All rights reserved under International and Pan-American Copyright Conventions. Published in the United States by Alfred A. Knopf, Inc., New York, and simultaneously in Canada by Random House of Canada Limited, Toronto. Distributed by Random House, Inc., New York.

Library of Congress Cataloging in Publication Data

Feiffer, Jules.
  Tantrum.
  Cartoons.
I. Title.
PN6727.F4T3   813'.5'4   79-2207
ISBN 0-394-50837-8

Manufactured in the United States of America
First Edition

TO

E.C. SEGAR
ROY CRANE
and
WILL EISNER

1

METAMORPHOSIS

15

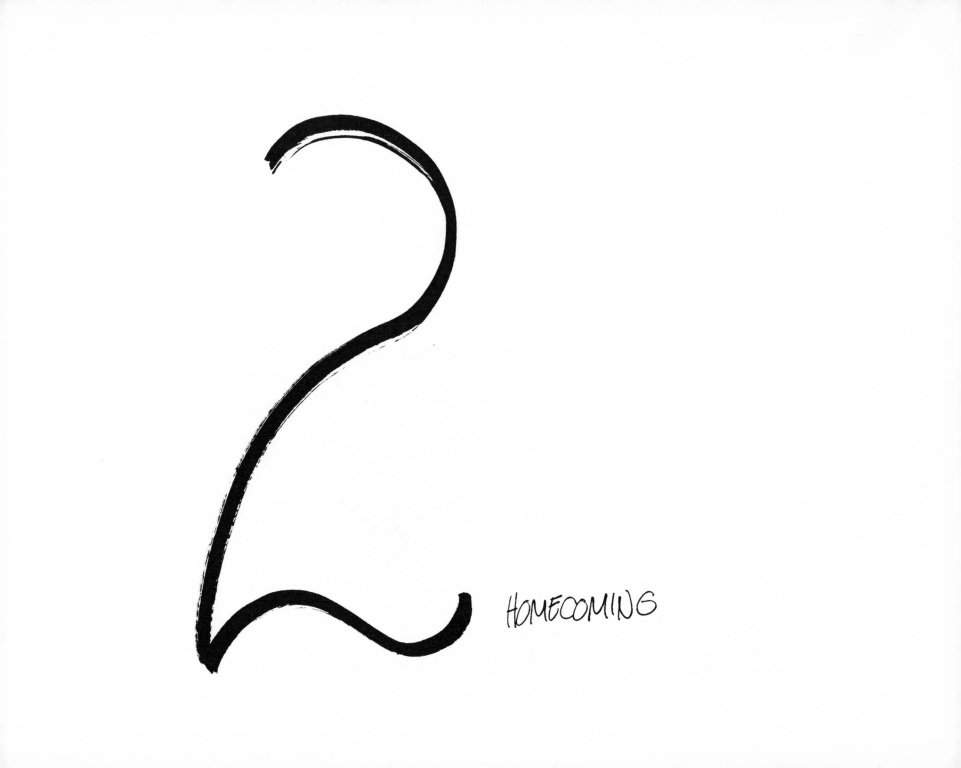

HOMECOMING

WE'RE OLD PEOPLE. WE'RE RETIRED. OUR CHILDREN ARE GROWN! OUT OF THE HOUSE! IN THE WORLD! WE HAVE NOTHING TO BE ASHAMED OF. GO AWAY!

28

38

plans

44

51

65

RESCUE

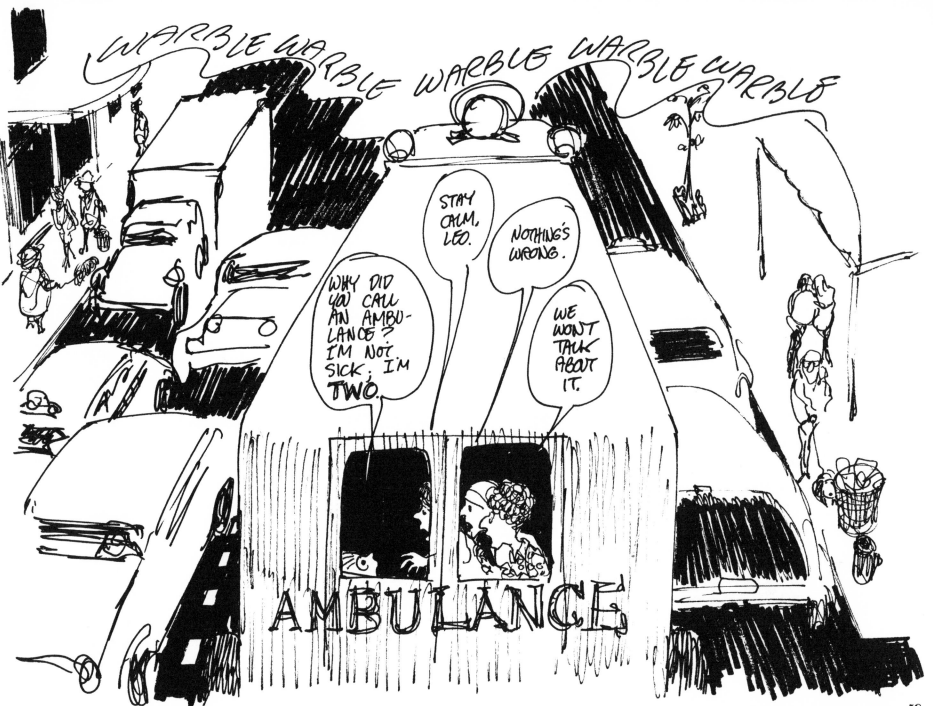

THE LAW

The Others

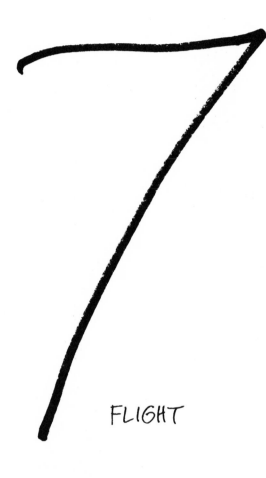

FLIGHT

BETRAYAL IS OUT THERE. TRICKINESS IS OUT THERE. IF I KNEW AT YOUR AGE WHAT I'VE LEARNED WITH GRIEF SINCE... DON'T THANK ME, JUST LISTEN:
FLIGHT 701 NOW BOARDING

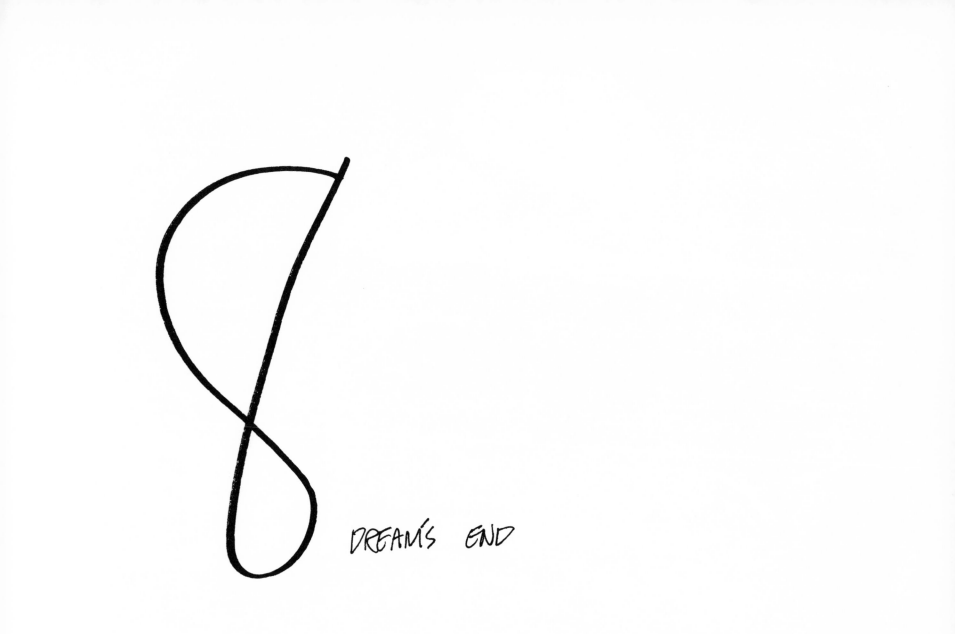

DREAM'S END

117

O, MY GOD, JOYCE! IS CHARLIE RESPONSIBLE FOR THIS? O, MY GOD!
GO FIND YOUR MOTHER, LITTLE BOY. I'M PREOCCUPIED

AN ORANGE IS SHARP AND TANGY AND FRESH-TASTING AND ALIVE, WHICH YOU ARE BARELY. YOU NEED MEDICAL ATTENTION.
THAT WAS WONDERFULLY DESCRIPTIVE, LEO. IF I WEREN'T SO FAT I'D RUN OUT AND EAT ONE. IF I COULD GET UP. NOW DESCRIBE A MELON.

128

HELLO, MOMMA, I'VE GOT SOME HOT NEWS FOR YOU! YOUR FAVORITE, CHARLIE, YOUR GOLDEN BOY: HE'S A KILLER! A KILLER! A KILLER!
OFF THE LINE, YOU MANIAC! MY HUSBAND HAS A SORE THROAT!

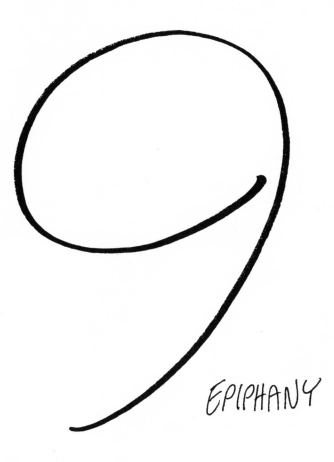

EPIPHANY

Leo,
I am off in the desert since it's more conducive to diet.
You'll find a color TV in the guest room.
I'll be back when I'm down to pure essence.
Sorry for the inconvenience.
As ever,
Joyce
O MY GOD!

144

EPIPHANY II

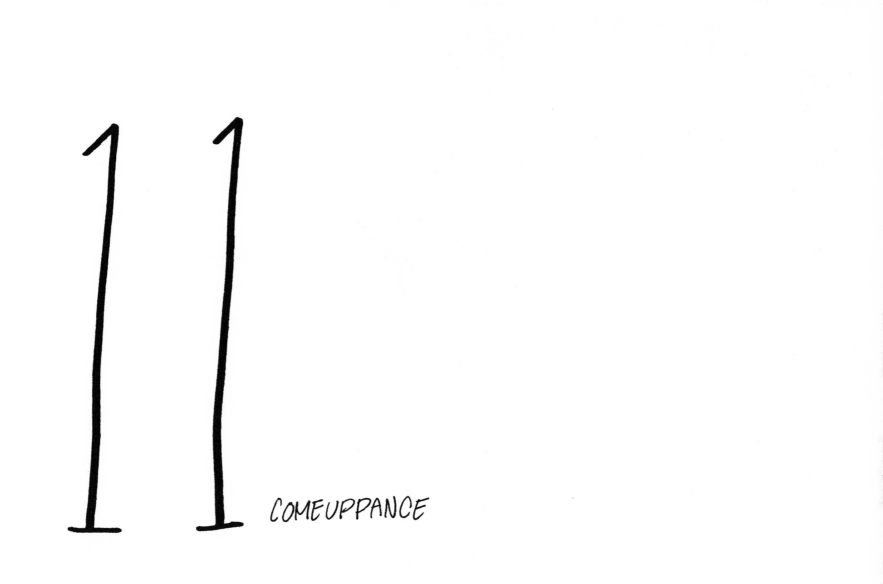

11 COMEUPPANCE

A Note on the Production of This Book

This book was printed by The Murray Printing Company, Forge Village, Massachusetts, and bound by the Sendor Bindery, New York, New York.

The paper is Mountie Vellum Opaque, made by Northwest Paper Company; it was supplied by Allan and Gray Paper Company.